P9-EMQ-817

Thanks for Giving

FOOD DRIVE!

HELP THOSE IN NEED
NOVEMBER 15 - 30

by ABBY KLEIN

illustrated by
JOHN McKINLEY

SCHOLASTIC INC.

New York   Toronto   London   Auckland
Sydney   Mexico City   New Delhi   Hong Kong

To my family. I am thankful for you every day. I love you!
—A.K.

To Bonnie with thanks.
—J.M.

ISBN-13: 978-0-545-14176-5
ISBN-10: 0-545-14176-1

Text copyright © 2009 by Abby Klein
Illustrations copyright © 2009 by John McKinley

12 11 10 9 8 7 6   14/0

Printed in the U.S.A.   40
First printing, October 2009

"Thanksgiving is next week," said our teacher, Mrs. Wushy.

She hung up a poster.

It said, "Food Drive."

"I can't wait to eat mashed potatoes," I said.
I rubbed my tummy. "Mmmmmm."
"My mom makes the best apple pie in the
whole world!" said Jessie.

"You are both nuts," said Max. "The best part of Thanksgiving is the turkey!"

"No, it is not!" said Chloe. "The best part is the stuffing."

"Turkey!" said Max.
"Stuffing!" said Chloe.
"Turkey!" said Max.
"Stuffing!" said Chloe.

"No fighting," said Mrs. Wushy.
"We should all be very thankful. We have
lots of food to eat on Thanksgiving."

"Some families do not have much to eat on Thanksgiving," said Mrs. Wushy. "We are going to help."

Mrs. Wushy pointed to the poster.

"Our school is having a food drive," said Mrs. Wushy.

"A what?" said Chloe.

"We bring in cans of food," said Robbie. "Then the school will give it to families who really need it."

"Cool!" I said.

On the bus ride home, Robbie said, "I am going to bring in lots of cans."

"Me, too," I said.

"I am going to bring in more than you!" said Chloe.

"I will bring in the most," said Max.

When I got home, I ran to the kitchen.
"Hello, Freddy," said my mom.
I pushed a chair over to the cabinet.
"Hi, Mom," I said.

I climbed on top of the chair and opened the cabinet.

"What are you doing, Freddy?" said my mom. "Get down right now!"

I got down off the chair.

"I need some food," I said.

"I can make you a snack," said my mom.

"I do not need a snack," I said. "I need food for the can drive at school."

"I can help you with that," said my mom.
She gave me a can of tuna fish and a can of corn.
"Thanks, Mom."

The next morning, my backpack was
really heavy.

I had to walk to class.

I could not run.

"Hey, Freddy."

Oh no! I knew that voice. It was Max. Max was the biggest bully in the whole first grade. I needed to get to class fast!

"Hey!" said Max.

He grabbed my arm.

What was he going to do to me?

Was he going to make fun of me?

Max followed me into the hallway.

"I need a favor," said Max.

"What?" I asked.

"I forgot to bring in a can of food,"
said Max. "Can I have one of yours?"

I just looked at him.

"You want one of my cans?" I said.

Max was always mean to me.

I did not want to help him.

So I lied.

"Sorry, Max," I said. "I do not have any extra cans."

"Really?" said Max.
"Really," I said.
Max looked down.
He let go of my arm.

Jessie and Robbie came running up to me.

"Are you okay?" Jessie asked.

"I am fine," I said.

"What did Max want?" said Robbie.

"Nothing," I said.

"Bring your cans to the rug," said
Mrs. Wushy. "Let me see what you have."

Everybody pulled their cans out of their backpacks.

"I have three cans of tuna fish," said Chloe.

"I have a can of potatoes and a can of peaches," said Robbie.

"I have a can of green beans and a can of corn," said Jessie.

I looked over at Max.
He was hiding behind a chair.
He looked very sad.
I felt sorry for him.

"Hey, Max," I whispered.

Max looked at me.

"Come over here," I said.

"Take this," I said.

I sneakily gave him one of my cans.

Max looked at me.

"But you said you did not have any extra cans," said Max.

"Well, I do," I said. "You can have one."
Max smiled. "Thanks, Freddy," he said.
"Sure," I said.

Mrs. Wushy tapped me on the shoulder.
"Do you boys have any cans?" she asked.
Max looked at me.
I looked at Max.
"Yes," we said.

"Now let's count the cans," said Mrs. Wushy.

We lined them up on the rug.

"We have five rows of ten cans," said Jessie.

"That is fifty cans," said Robbie.

"Wow! That is a lot of cans," said Chloe.

"It sure is," said Mrs. Wushy.

"Now a lot of families will have a very happy Thanksgiving," said Max.